FALLING

A STARRY KNIGHT EPISODE OF
THE STARTLIGHT CHRONICLES

A GRAPHIC NOVEL

STORY BY
C. S. Johnson

ART BY
Eko Bambang

STORY AUTHOR
C. S. Johnson

ILLUSTRATOR
Eko Bambang

Print ISBN:

For Sam.

Story adapted from *Falling: A Starry Knight Episode of The Starlight Chronicles* by C. S. Johnson, part of the short story collection from The Starlight Chronicles. The story is set between books 2 and 3.

This book includes a sample chapter of *Beauty's Curse*, Book 1 of C. S. Johnson's *Once Upon a Princess Saga*.

I HAVE SPENT A GOOD DEAL OF MY LIFE COMING TO TERMS WITH DEATH. TODAY IS NO EXCEPTION, I TOLD MYSELF. SIGHING, I LOOKED DOWN FROM THE ROOF OF RACHEL'S CAFE, GLAD THE FADING EVENING LIGHT WAS ABLE TO HIDE MY GLUM EXPRESSION FROM THE PASSERSBY BELOW.

DID IT REALLY MATTER IF THE TERMS HAD CHANGED SINCE I'D STARTED DOWN THIS PATH? YES. DON'T KID YOURSELF.

I SIGHED. THE MIDNIGHT CROWD WAS BEGINNING TO CRAWL INTO THE SMALL COFFEEHOUSE AND RESTAURANT BELOW, LOOKING FOR WARMTH FROM THE LINGERING CHILL IN THE AIR AND COMFORT FROM THE LASTING TROUBLES OF THE DAY.

THE IRONY OF MY SITUATION WAS NOT LOST ON ME; PEOPLE WOULD COME INTO THE BUSINESS UNDER MY HOME EVERY DAY TO FIND PEACE, WHILE ITS GENEROSITY IN THIS MATTER WOULD NEVER EXTEND TO ME.

I KNEW LIFE WAS HARD, AND I HAD NO RIGHT TO COMPLAIN. BUT IT WASN'T SUPPOSED TO BE LIKE THIS. I SHOULD HAVE SEEN THIS POSSIBILITY, I CHIDED MYSELF SILENTLY. I SHOULD HAVE KNOWN. I SMIRKED TO MYSELF IN RESIGNATION; KNOWING DID NOTHING TO MAKE IT BETTER. IN FACT, I WAS FAIRLY SURE IT MADE IT WORSE.

MY PALMS, STRETCHED OUT BEFORE ME, GRAPPLED WITH THE CEMENT BARRIER, THE ONLY THING BETWEEN ME AND FALLING. ALTHOUGH, I THOUGHT PLAYFULLY AS I STOOD THERE, IT DIDN'T MATTER MUCH IF I DID OR NOT. I HAD NEVER BEEN AFRAID OF FALLING BEFORE, AND I HAD NEVER BEEN AFRAID OF DEATH BEFORE.

BEFORE ... BEFORE I REALIZED— I SQUEEZED MY EYES SHUT, TRYING TO BLOCK OUT MY THOUGHTS. I DIDN'T WANT TO THINK ABOUT IT. I COULDN'T THINK ABOUT IT, AND BECAUSE I COULDN'T, I COULDN'T MOVE PAST IT.

MAYBE I DIDN'T WANT TO MOVE PAST IT. THERE WAS A WHISPER IN THE WIND OF THE NIGHT; THE CITY RUMBLED OUT ITS OWN BEAT, WHILE THE STARS ABOVE FLIRTED FREELY WITH THE IMPOUNDING DARKNESS SURROUNDING THEM. MY FINGERS SCRAPPED AGAINST THE COOL, GRAY CEMENT OF THE BUILDING LEDGE AS I CURLED THEM INTO FISTS. I WATCHED THEM, MY HANDS SEEMING UNUSUALLY SMALL AND INSTINCTIVELY ALIEN. FOR ONCE, MY LONG HAIR FLEW FREE OF ITS BINDING; THE CURLING ENDS OF MY GINGERBREAD HAIR LICKED AT MY ARMS, OFFERING ONLY A TEASING WARMTH FOR COMFORT.

MY EYES DRIFTED FROM MY FISTS TO THE UNDERSIDE OF MY RIGHT WRIST WHERE, UNDER A BRACELET RACHEL HAD MADE FOR ME WHEN I'D FIRST COME TO LIVE WITH HER TEN YEARS AGO, A SILVER FOURPOINT STAR SHIMMERED ALONG WITH THE STARLIGHT.

AS IF ON CUE, I COULD SUDDENLY FEEL MALEVOLENT POWER VIBRATING THROUGH THE LABYRINTHINE CITY STREETS. I SHIFTED UNCOMFORTABLY, KNOWING IT WOULDN'T BE LONG BEFORE THE DEMONIC ENTITY WOULD MAKE ITS WAY TO ME; EVENTUALLY THEY ALL CAME TO FIND ME.

I SUPPOSE IT IS THE KIND OF EVENING STARRY KNIGHT COULD APPRECIATE, I MUSED, GRINNING TO MYSELF; MY OWN ALTER EGO WAS MORE OF AN INSIDE JOKE TO ME, RATHER THAN A SECRET HALF OF MY IDENTITY.

THE TRICK, I KNEW FROM EXPERIENCE, WAS TO BE PREPARED.

HIYAAA...

I MOVED THE BRACELET BACK AND PRESSED INTO THE NOW-GLOWING MARK, AND FELT A WAVE OF FIRE COURSE THROUGH MY BODY AS A PAIR OF WINGS BLOSOMED OUT OF MY BACK AND ANOTHER PAIR CROWNED ACROSS MY FOREHEAD.

LOOKING UP TO THE SLIVER OF MOONLIGHT ABOVE THE APOLLO CITY SKYLINE, I FOUGHT THE OVERWHELMING TEMPTATION TO SHUDDER.

IT WAS LIKE THIS TEN YEARS AGO

I WHISPERED TO MYSELF. THE MOON HAD BEEN AN EVIL SMIRK IN THE SKY THE NIGHT MY PARENTS HAD DIED.

EVERY SECOND BROUGHT ME CLOSER TO ITS DEATH IN THIS WORLD.

SOON, THE PULSING SENSATION IN MY ARM BURNED, SIGNALING I WAS CLOSE. MY HEART, AS TWISTED AND BROKEN AS IT WAS IN ITS FORM, HUMMED WITH BLATANT ASSURANCE AS IT TOOK ME CLOSER TO MY PREY WITH EVERY BEAT. I WAS GETTING CLOSER TO MY TARGET.

CRINK!!!

THE BOW OF RIGHTEOUSNESS

ESPECIALLY FOR ME, ESPECIALLY AT NIGHT. IT WAS TOO EASY TO SINK BACK INTO THE PAST, BACK TO THE NIGHT MY PARENTS DIED.

REMEMBERED THE COLD STRIPS OF WATER FLOGGING MY SEVEN-YEAROLD SELF AS THE CAR TUMBLED INTO THE DARK DEPTHS, STAYING THERE UNTIL STILLNESS. THAT NIGHT, THE WATER BELOW THE HIGHWAY HAD TAKEN THE LIFE OF MY MOTHER AND FATHER, SPITTING ME BACK OUT.

DEATH HAD BEGUN ITS CONSTANT PARADE IN MY LIFE. AND EVER SINCE THEN, NIGHT HAD BEEN DEATH'S PREFERRED HUNTING GROUND. ALTHOUGH, I MUSED TO MYSELF IN A MOMENT OF WEAKNESS, THAT WAS NOT ALL THAT HAPPENED THAT NIGHT. MY EYES INVOLUNTARILY SLIPPED TO THE EMBLEM OF THE PRINCE ON MY WRIST.

AND I HAD BEEN MARKED FOR A NEW PURPOSE, WHILE SCORCHED BY AN OLD LIFE. THAT WAS WHAT I FOUND MYSELF WITH VERY SHORTLY—A SENSE OF NEWNESS FORGED ALONGSIDE AN ANCIENT AND ETERNAL CALLING. I HAD A NEW BODY WITH OLD MEMORIES, A NEW CHANCE WITH OLD ENEMIES—I WAS A FALLEN STAR, AN ASTRONESHAMA; YET SOMEHOW STILL A STAR BUT ONE WITH NO TRUE LIGHT TO SHINE.

FINALLY I SUCCUMBED TO MY FEAR AND TREMBLED. SO MUCH HAD CHANGED WHEN DEATH CAME, I THOUGHT, WRAPPING MY ARMS AROUND MYSELF MORE TIGHTLY.

I'M NOT SURE SHE'S KEEN ON KEEPING HER PROMISE IN THAT REGARD, ESPECIALLY SINCE YOUR FRIEND HAS BEEN BLOGGING ABOUT THIS ENTIRE ADVENTURE.

MIKEY WANTED THE BLOG TO MAKE MONEY FOR COLLEGE

A STRANGE SENSE OF APPROVAL FLUTTERED THROUGH MY HEART. IT WAS SWEET OF HIM TO DEFEND HIS FRIEND. ALTHOUGH HIS FRIEND WAS PROBABLY PUTTING HIMSELF IN QUITE A BIT OF DANGER BY BLOGGING ABOUT OUR SUPERNATURAL ENTANGLEMENTS. I TIGHTENED MY HAND AROUND MY BOW. THE HUMMING OF THE ONCOMING DEMON WAS GETTING CLOSER. IT WOULDN'T BE MUCH LONGER, I THOUGHT.

KID, COLLEGE WASN'T ALWAYS AROUND. DO YOU REALLY THINK IT'LL BE HERE IN ANOTHER TWO HUNDRED YEARS?

UGH, GIVE IT A REST, ELYSIAN ... I'M MORE WORRIED ABOUT SWORD THAN STARRY KNIGHT.

WHY?

ELYSIAN SWIVELED HIS HEAD AROUND. HE JUMPED BACK TO WINGDINGER'S SIDE, FLYING A SMALL DISTANCE OFF THE GROUND.

HIS OWN BAT-LIKE WINGS MELTED INTO THE SHADOWS, MAKING IT HARD FOR EVEN ME TO SEE HIS EXACT POSITION AND FORM. I PURSED MY LIPS IN RELUCTANT ADMIRATION; I KNEW ELYSIAN WAS A CHANGELING DRAGON, AND THERE WERE ONLY A FEW DRAGONS OF THAT CALIBER ON THE OTHER SIDE OF TIME.

IT'S NONE OF YOUR BUSINESS

ELYSIAN SNARLED AND TOOK OFF FOR HIGHER SKIES AT THE REPROACH; INSTINCTIVELY, I STEPPED FURTHER BACK INTO THE SHADOWS.

I WONDERED WHY I WAS NOT AS MUCH AS A THREAT AS ELYSIAN–AND I–WOULD PREFER HIM TO THINK.

AS IF IN ANSWERING MY UNSPOKEN QUERY, MY CO-DEFENDER WENT STILL. HIS BLUE EYES, A CRYSTALLINE BLUE, GLAZED OVER, AND HIS FINGERS GRAZED LIGHTLY OVER HIS LIPS.

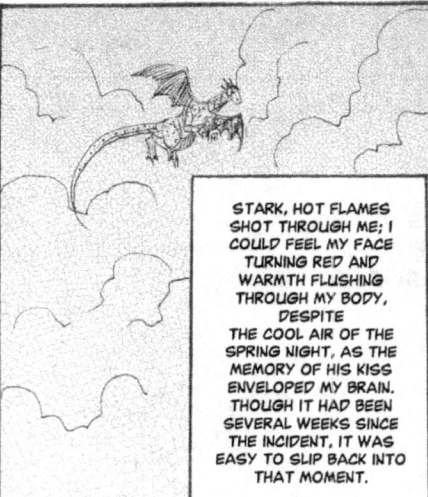

STARK, HOT FLAMES SHOT THROUGH ME; I COULD FEEL MY FACE TURNING RED AND WARMTH FLUSHING THROUGH MY BODY, DESPITE THE COOL AIR OF THE SPRING NIGHT, AS THE MEMORY OF HIS KISS ENVELOPED MY BRAIN. THOUGH IT HAD BEEN SEVERAL WEEKS SINCE THE INCIDENT, IT WAS EASY TO SLIP BACK INTO THAT MOMENT.

RECALLING THE URGENT PRESSURE OF HIS MOUTH ON MINE, THE WAY HE'D GENTLY CRADLED MY FACE AND HELD BACK MY HAIR, I FELT MY HEARTBEAT ACCELERATE, EVEN AS IT STOPPED; MY HANDS STARTED SHAKING AGAIN, THOUGH IN FURIOUS PROTEST OR TACIT PLEASURE, I COULD NOT SAY. DON'T DO THIS TO YOURSELF.

I HATE THIS

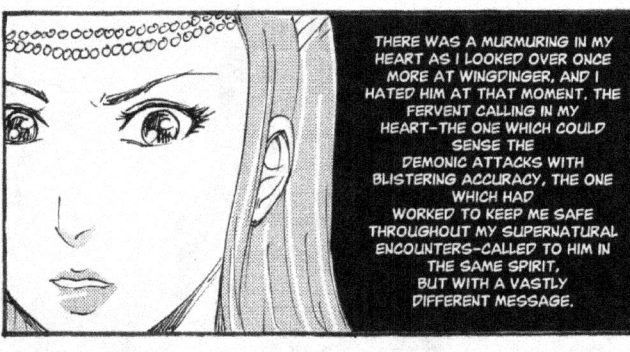

THERE WAS A MURMURING IN MY HEART AS I LOOKED OVER ONCE MORE AT WINGDINGER, AND I HATED HIM AT THAT MOMENT. THE FERVENT CALLING IN MY HEART—THE ONE WHICH COULD SENSE THE DEMONIC ATTACKS WITH BLISTERING ACCURACY, THE ONE WHICH HAD WORKED TO KEEP ME SAFE THROUGHOUT MY SUPERNATURAL ENCOUNTERS—CALLED TO HIM IN THE SAME SPIRIT, BUT WITH A VASTLY DIFFERENT MESSAGE.

THE SURGE TO PROTECT, THE DESIRE TO PROVIDE, THE SURENESS OF PROMISE ... ALL OF IT WOUND ITS WAY AROUND ME, ENCOMPASSING ME, KNITTING ITSELF TO MY IDENTITY, HOUSING ITSELF IN THE CORE OF MY BEING.

IT ANGERED ME THAT I WOULD NEVER BE ABLE TO SEPARATE WHO I WAS FROM THIS BOY. I WATCHED AS HE TRIED TO TAKE OFF HIMSELF, SHAKING HIS WINGS BUT NEVER LEAVING THE GROUND. HE CURSED A FEW TIMES, AND THEN CALLED OUT FOR ELYSIAN.

IT ANGERED ME EVEN MORE HE WAS AN IDIOT, LARGELY IGNORANT OF HIS POWER AND EGOTISTICAL TO A FAULT. HIS SELF-CENTERED SHOWMANSHIP DISGUSTED ME, AND HE RESERVED HIS LOVE FOR HIMSELF. I FELT THE GRIP ON MY BOW TIGHTEN.

THAT'S NOT ALL TRUE ... I KNEW I WASN'T BEING FAIR; I WAS FURIOUSLY FRUSTRATED. BUT I DIDN'T WANT TO THINK ABOUT THAT. IT WAS MUCH EASIER TO SEE HIM AS A MISTAKE, A BUMBLING FORM OF COLLATERAL DAMAGE, SOMETHING I HAD TO DISREGARD.

IT WAS DEFINITELY MUCH EASIER TO OVERLOOK HIM IN THEORY THAN IN PRACTICE.

FROM THE MOMENT I'D SEEN HIM AT APOLLO CENTRAL'S PLAY PRACTICE, ALL THOSE MONTHS AGO, I WAS UNABLE TO IGNORE HIM. EVEN IN HIS HUMAN FORM, I WOULD HAVE KNOWN HIM ANYWHERE. FINDING HIM CROUCHING OVER MY WORK ON THE STAGE, LOOKING DOWN AS HE HAD ADMIRED MY WORK ON THE BACKDROP, IT WAS TOO SURREAL.

IT DIDN'T TAKE ME LONG TO REALIZE HE DIDN'T KNOW ME, BUT IT WAS REASSURING TO SEE THAT OVER THE FOLLOWING MONTHS AND BRIEF ENCOUNTERS WITH HIM AS STARRY KNIGHT.

AN UNCONSCIOUS SMILE PLAYED ON MY LIPS, AS I RECALLED THE MOMENT I'D SEEN HIM, MY FIRST DAY AS A TRANSFER STUDENT FROM ROSEMONT. IT HAD BEEN THE FIRST TIME I'D SPOKEN TO HIM AS MY REGULAR SELF, AND IT HAD PROVED TO BE JUST AS HARD TO DEAL WITH HIM AS A STARLIGHT WARRIOR AS IT WAS AS A HUMAN.

IT WAS FOR THE BEST, I REMINDED MYSELF. I DIDN'T LIKE HAVING TO DEAL WITH HIM, BUT IT HELPED HE WAS DATING GWEN KESSLER, WHO I BEFRIENDED AT THE PLAY PRODUCTION.

THE LANCE OF PAIN AND UNCERTAINTY IN MY HEART ALLOWED IT TO BEAT REGULARLY AGAIN. MY HEAD SLUMPED INTO MY HANDS IN HELPLESS DERISION. NOT TO MENTION WERE OTHER COMPLICATIONS AS WELL, I RECALLED, THINKING OF HIS BROTHER, AND HIS PARENTS. I STRAIGHTENED UP. NO, OUR RELATIONSHIP WOULD NEVER BE EASY, AND IT WAS FOR THE BEST. HAMILTON HAD A CHANCE TO BE HAPPY AND FREE, AND I COULDN'T IGNORE THAT.

ESPECIALLY WHEN HE WAS SO DIFFICULT TO DEAL WITH ON THE BATTLEFIELD. THE REASON IN MY MIND WAS QUICKLY SQUASHED BY THE TREMORS IN MY BLOOD.

TIME TO GET TO WORK

WHO'S THERE?

IT'S ME

OH

NICE TO SEE YOU, TOO

CAN YOU TELL WHERE THE DEMON IS? ITS AURA IS HERE BUT I DON'T ACTUALLY SEE IT

IT'S CIRCLING

I GLANCED AROUND. THERE WAS A BURNING TRAIL OF DEMONIC POWER ALL SURROUNDING US, BUT IT WASN'T VISIBLE. I WAS JUST ABOUT TO ASK IF ELYSIAN HAD BEEN ABLE TO SEE ANYTHING EARLIER WHEN A RINGTONE BROKE MY CONCENTRATION.

TELL HIM I DON'T WANT TO HAVE TO WORRY ABOUT HIM IN ADDITION TO YOU

I KNOW IT'S NOT IDEAL, BUT AT LEAST I HAVE FRIENDS

I MUST BE A TERRIBLE FRIEND INDEED, IF I INSIST ON KEEPING THEM AWAY FROM THE BATTLEFIELD

HE IS AWAY FROM THE BATTLEFIELD

I WAS JUST TALKING TO HIM ON THE PHONE

OUCH!

YES, THAT'S FINE. IF IT'LL MAKE YOU FEEL BETTER,

COOL. THAT'S A GOOD IDEA. I THINK I'LL DO THAT.

FINE, JUST START HELPING ME OUT HERE.

GOTCHA,

FWOOOSS..

ZUUU...

DHUUAAARRR!

AAARRGGGGGH!

BRAAKH!!!

ARE YOU OKAY?

I WATCHED HIM FOR A MOMENT BEFORE TUNING BACK INTO THE TENWALEISK'S POWER. I SLUMPED OVER; IT WAS STILL CLOSE BY, BUT IT WAS IN HIDING. ELYSIAN GROWLED BEHIND ME, AND I TENTATIVELY HEADED OVER. IF I COULDN'T VANQUISH EVIL, I FIGURED I SHOULD SEE IF I CAN DO SOME GOOD.

YOU SURE YOU'RE OKAY?

I'LL BE FINE,

IN A LITTLE BIT.

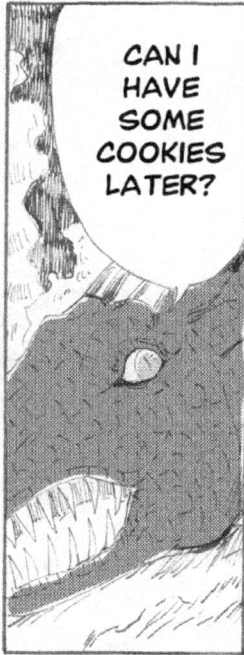

CAN I HAVE SOME COOKIES LATER?

UGH, YOU ARE ANNOYING,

I'LL HAVE TO GET MORE FROM RACHEL. CHERYL'S STILL ON HER MEAT-HEAVY, SUGARFREE CLEANSING DIET.

WE NEED A PLAN.

NO KIDDING,

HE'S USING THE ELECTRICAL CABLES,

HE'S STILL CLOSE BY, SO HE COULD ATTACK AGAIN SOON.

HE WAS IN MY CELL PHONE, SO HE'S NOT JUST IN THE PHONE LINES; HE'S IN THE TELECOMMUNI-CATION SYSTEMS.

WE NEED TO ISOLATE HIM AND THEN DESTROY HIM. DO YOU THINK WE CAN DO THAT WITH THE WIRES HERE?

WE'D HAVE TO DRAW HIM OUT OF THEM AGAIN.

I CAN KNOCK A FEW OF THOSE POLES DOWN, IF YOU GIVE ME A FEW MOMENTS.

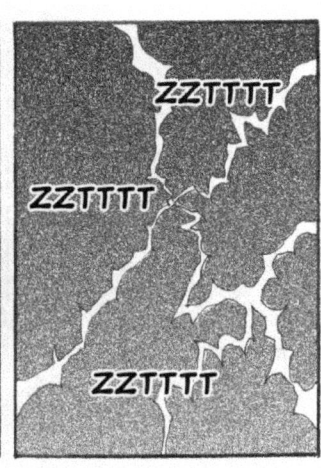

ZZTTTT

ZZTTTT

ZZTTTT

HE'S COMING BACK, WE HAVE TO HURRY.

IS THERE A WAY WE CAN SHUT DOWN THE POWER FOR A FEW MOMENTS?

I KNOW THAT SOUNDS PRETTY EASY, BUT SHORT OF FINDING THE NEAREST CITY ELECTRIC GENERATOR, WE'RE NOT GOING TO HAVE A LOT OF LUCK, WHICH WE WOULD ALSO NEED.

HOW WOULD YOU DO IT THEN?I SUPPOSE YOU ACTUALLY PAID ATTENTION IN MR. H—

I MEAN, MR. ELECTRICITY GUY'S SCIENCE CLASS?

TSHKA!

TSHKA!

WHAT?

I HAVE AN IDEA.

TSHKA!

WHAT IS IT?

YOU CAN CREATE A SMALL SUPERNOVA, RIGHT?

TSHKA!

I ALREADY DON'T LIKE THE SOUND OF THIS.

NO, LISTEN TO ME. WE'LL GET ELYSIAN TO LEAD HIM TO THIS INTERSECTION.

AW,

THEN, ONCE IT'S HERE, YOU'LL GIVE OFF A SURGE OF POWER, AND RUN HIM OUT. THEN I'LL MAKE SURE HE'S TAKEN CARE OF.

HOW WILL THAT WORK?

IF YOU OVERLOAD THE POWER CIRCUITS, IT'LL TRIGGER A SMALL POWER OUTAGE.

IT'S A SUPERNOVA; IT'S NOT EXACTLY A SMALL SOLUTION.

IT'S A QUICK SOLUTION WHICH DOESN'T INVOLVE US HUNTING ALL OVER THE CITY AND DISMANTLED GOVERNMENT PROPERTY. ALSO, THE EQUIPMENT SHOULD BE FINE. IT'S JUST LIKE A POWER SURGE, RIGHT?

WHAT IF I CAN'T STOP IT?

ELYSIAN, GO OFF AND LURE THE TEN-WA-LISK THING THIS WAY. WE'LL BE READY FOR HIM.

TENWA-LEISK,

OH, COME ON, KID ...

NOW, JUST GO. GO AND I'LL GET YOUR GOOFY COOKIES FOR YOU.

FINE. BUT I WANT AT LEAST A DOZEN.

FINE.

AND HE SAYS I HAVE PROBLEMS WITH COMMIT-MENT.

ELYSIAN'S ALWAYS BEEN ONE TO SEE OTHER PEOPLE'S WEAKNESSES. IT'S A GOOD THING, AND IT'S A TERRIBLE THING.

AGREED,

OUR EYES MET AND WE BOTH WENT SILENT. THEN, AVOIDING THE AWKWARD SILENCE, I RESUMED MY DEBATE STANCE.

YOU NEVER ANSWERED MY QUESTION. WHAT WILL HAPPEN IF I CAN'T STOP THE SUPERNOVA?

I'LL BE HERE TO STOP YOU,

SHUT UP,

MY PLEASURE.

I'LL BE OVER HERE.

I CAN'T BELIEVE I AGREED TO DO THIS. BUT HAMILTON GAVE ME A SMALL SMILE BEFORE HE DUCKED BEHIND A CORNER, AND I KNEW AT THAT MOMENT THERE REALLY WAS NO WONDER WHY I WAS IN MY POSITON.

OKAY.

BUT THERE WERE OTHER REASONS, TOO. AFTER ALL, HAMILTON WAS THE SMARTEST KID IN MY CLASS, AND I HADN'T REALLY PAID MUCH ATTENTION TO MR. HALE'S LECTURES; BETWEEN THE TWO OF US, HE WAS THE ONE WHO MORE LIKELY TO KNOW ABOUT ELECTRICAL POWER AND ITS CHANNELS AND WHATEVER ELSE THERE WAS TO WORRY ABOUT. AS I HEARD ELYSIAN ROAR IN THE DISTANCE, I MADE A SILENT VOW I WOULD PAY MORE ATTENTION TO THE CLASSWORK IN THE FUTURE.

WE'RE COMING!

WAIT TILL HE GETS TO THIS INTERSECTION, AND THEN POWER UP,

WE'LL CUT HIM OFF RIGHT HERE, AND HE'LL BE WITHIN REACH.

FINE.

TSHKA! TSHKA!

SUPERNOVA!!

UH-OH.

NO!

HIYAAAA....

WHAT ARE YOU DOING, STARRY KNIGHT?

THE POWER LINES CACKLED AND
SNAPPED AROUND US, AND THE
WOODEN POLES BECAME LIKE
LIGHTNING POLES, STRIKING OUT
MY EXTRA POWER THROUGHOUT
THE SKIES. SUDDENLY, I WAS
STRONGLY REMINDED OF THE
FIRST TIME I HAD EVER USED MY
POWER.

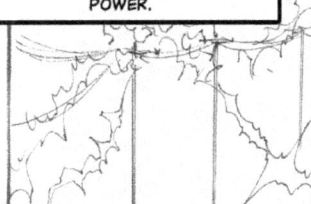

HIYAAA

HIYAAAA...

AAAAAARGGG....

DHUAR!

THE TENWALEISK SUDDENLY
GROANED AND BURST, AS
MY POWER OVERCAME HIS
PHYSICAL LIMITATIONS.

FOR A SPLIT SECOND I REJOICED, SINCE HE WAS GONE; BUT IN THE NEXT, I WAS THROWN INTO FEAR AS MY POWER NEVER FALTERED. IT'S HAPPENING AGAIN, ONLY THIS TIME, THE SINISTERS ARE NOWHERE NEAR. I HAVE TO STOP THIS. I HAVE TO SAVE EVERYONE. WARMTH CRAWLED FROM MY HAND, UNABLE TO MOVE, I STOOD THERE, STILL, WONDERING WHAT WAS HAPPENING. WAS I GOING TO BREAK OPEN THE SPACE-TIME CONTINUUM AGAIN? THE SUPERNOVA POWER WAS RAW AND UNTRIED, AND I FELT THE TEMPTATION TO LET IT GO FURTHER.

STARRY KNIGHT!

WUSS...

I ALMOST EXPECTED TO SEE ADONAIAS' KIND FACE GAZING AT ME, THE WORDS OF TERROR AND COMFORT RINGING THROUGH MY HEART'S MEMORY

I AM WAITING FOR YOU.

HE WANTS TO KISS ME AGAIN.

WHAT HAPPENED?

THE MONSTER, UM, HE TRIED TO GAIN MORE POWER BY TAKING YOURS, AND HE BLEW UP AS A RESULT.

ELYSIAN FLEW AWAY AGAIN. MY GUESS IS HE DIDN'T WANT TO GET SUCKED INTO YOUR NOVA WHIRLWIND.

I GUESS THAT'S A LEGITIMATE CONCERN, SINCE HE WAS INJURED,

WE GOT THE DEMON,

YEAH.

WELL, IF THAT'S THE CASE, I'M GOING TO GO,

AFTER MIDNIGHT, SO ...

OKAY.

I HURRIED OFF, WITHOUT SAYING ANOTHER WORD. I HURRIED OFF AND TOOK FLIGHT, TRYING NOT TO THINK ABOUT THE TEARS THAT FLECKED MY VISION, OR HOW MUCH I HOPED I DIDN'T START LIVING FOR THE DAY WHEN HE WOULD KISS ME AGAIN.

I WAS OKAY WITH DEATH. I WAS. I'D BEEN SURROUNDED BY IT NEARLY ALL MY LIFE. I KNEW THE PAIN IT CAUSED, AND I KNEW HOW HARD IT WAS TO KEEP FIGHTING SOME DAYS. IT WAS A FAMILIAR FRIEND IN THIS BUSINESS. SO WHY WAS I SO UPSET THAT THESE LAST FEW MONTHS, I'D BEEN CONTEMPLATING LIFE MORE THAN DEATH?

YOU'RE LATER THAN I THOUGHT

IT WAS A TENWALEISK. THEY'RE SOMETIMES TRICKY TO KILL.

ESPECIALLY IF YOU DON'T WANT TO MAKE A RUCKUS, THERE WAS A POWER OUTAGE OVER IN THE WESTERN PART OF THE CITY.

YEAH.

DID YOU GET HELP FROM THAT WINGDINGER FELLOW, AND HIS PET DRAGON?

SOMEHOW, I DIDN'T THINK ELYSIAN WOULD LIKE TO BE REFERRED TO AS A PET. BUT I DIDN'T BOTHER TO CORRECT GRANDPA'S ASSUMPTIONS. IF THERE WAS ANYONE I OWED IN THIS WORLD, IT WAS GRANDPA. AFTER MY PARENTS HAD BEEN KILLED, HE'D BEEN THE FIRST ONE TO COME AND GET ME. IT WAS HIS SON, AFTER ALL, AND HIS WIFE WHO HAD DIED; I'D NEVER MET HIM PRIOR TO THE ACCIDENT, BUT MY PARENTS HAD NO WILL, AND IT WAS SHORTLY AFTER GRANDPA CAME AND GOT ME, WE BOTH WOUND UP RELOCATING TO APOLLO CITY TO LIVE WITH RACHEL AND HER MOTHER, LETICIA.

DID HE GIVE YOU ANY TROUBLE, RAIYA?

NO, HE'S GETTING STRONGER.

WELL, THAT'S GOOD TO HEAR.

ARE YOU GOING TO TELL HIM WE KNOW ABOUT HIM? WILL YOU TEACH HIM, LIKE YOU TAUGHT ME?

ELYSIAN HAS APPOINTED HIMSELF THE MENTOR. I DOUBT I WILL NEED TO STEP IN. CHANGELING DRAGONS ARE QUITE POWERFUL.

DON'T YOU THINK WE SHOULD TELL HIM THOUGH? I MEAN, IF HE'S REALLY DEDICATED NOW?

"I'M NOT SURE I AM READY TO TRUST THIS FELLOW, RAIYA. HE'S PROVEN HIMSELF MORE HINDRANCE THAN HELP. AND HE'S STILL YOUNG IN THIS PATH. I'VE ASKED YOU NOT TO REVEAL ME FOR GOOD REASON, AND I APPRECIATE YOUR SILENCE ON THE MATTER.

I THOUGHT YOU JUST WANTED ME NOT TO SAY ANYTHING SO YOU COULD TEASE HIM,

WELL, THAT'S GREAT FUN, TO BE SURE, BUT THERE ARE TIMES WHEN WE MUST ACT—AS I DID IN BRINGING YOU TO LIVE HERE—AND THERE ARE TIMES WHEN WE ARE CALLED TO SILENCE. I HAVE NOT FELT THE PRESS TO ACTION. NOT JUST YET, ANYWAY.

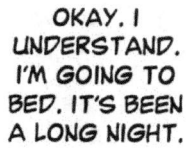

OKAY. I UNDERSTAND. I'M GOING TO BED. IT'S BEEN A LONG NIGHT.

I'LL SAY. OH, BEFORE YOU GO, RACHEL WAS HOPING TO TALK TO YOU.

OKAY.

YES, GRANDPA?

RAIYA.

THAT WAS QUICK THINKING TONIGHT ON YOUR PART. I AM PROUD OF YOU, AND YOUR PARENTS WOULD BE, TOO.

THANKS.

OH? ARE YOU GOING TO DO SOME MOONSCAPES FOR ME SOON?

RAIYA! WHERE DID YOU GET OFF TO, THIS LATE AT NIGHT?

JUST WENT OUT FOR A BIT. I WAS CHECKING OUT THE MOON A BIT,

THERE WAS A MERCENARY GLEAM IN HER EYE, BUT I COULD FORGIVE RACHEL FOR ANYTHING. SHE WAS MORE THAN MY COUSIN; SHE WAS MY BEST FRIEND, AND WHILE SHE DIDN'T KNOW I WAS SECRETLY A SUPERHERO AND FALLEN STAR, SHE WAS THE ONE WHO, ALL THOSE YEARS AGO, HAD SUGGESTED ART THERAPY AS AN ANSWER FOR MY DEPRESSION. FOLLOWING MY PARENTS' DEATHS, I HAD TAKEN UP ART WITH GREAT PASSION, AND IT STILL NEVER CEASED TO BRING ME HOME WHEN I WAS FEELING BLUE.

MAYBE, IS THAT WHAT YOU WANTED TO ASK ME ABOUT?

NO, I WAS WONDERING IF YOU WOULD PLAY SOMETHING SPECIAL FOR ME AND LEE AT OUR WEDDING.

WHEW. GLAD THAT'S DONE.

I MADE SOME COCOA EARLIER. WANT ANY?

SURE,

HA...
HA...
HA....

I WOULDN'T SAY THAT I WAS A STAR ALWAYS BURNS BRIGHTEST BEFORE IT DIES.

YOU'VE ALWAYS BEEN STUBBORN, I ALWAYS LOSE TO YOU.

AND YOU WILL NOT WIN AGAINST ME NEXT TIME, EITHER. BUT DON'T WORRY. I'LL BE AROUND FOR YOUR WEDDING. I'D BE HAPPY TO PLAY SOMETHING FOR YOU.

I WAS THINKING OF MAKING MY OWN CAKE. DO YOU THINK YOU'D WANT TO HELP WITH THAT?

JASON MIGHT BE A BETTER CANDIDATE FOR THE JOB,

THE ONLY THINGS I'M REALLY GOOD AT MAKING ARE MY CHOCOLATE CHIP GINGERBREAD COOKIES.

THAT'S NOT A BAD IDEA, I WAS THINKING OF GETTING HIM TO HELP ME WITH CATERING, I'M SURE HE'D LOVE THAT.

WE TALKED FOR A BIT LONGER OF RACHEL'S PLANS TO EXPAND HER BUSINESS, WORKING WITH BAKERY SWEETS AND COOKING FOR HIGHEREND CATERING.

WARMED BY HER CONVERSATION, BOTH LIGHT AND MEANINGFUL, I HEADED UP TO MY ROOM WITH A SENSE OF PURPOSE. IT WAS TRULY AN HONOR FOR ME TO KNOW RACHEL AS A SISTER, AND HELP MAKE HER WEDDING DAY SPECIAL. I CAUGHT SIGHT OF THE EMBLEM OF THE PRINCE ON MY WRIST AND, NOT FOR THE FIRST TIME LATELY, UNCERTAINTY STRUCK ME. I OPENED UP THE WINDOW IN MY ROOM, AND LEANED OUT, LOOKING AT THE NIGHT SKY.

IT DIDN'T MATTER IF I HAD A FAMILY I LOVED, OR EVEN IF I'D FALLEN IN LOVE. I WAS A FALLEN STAR; I HAD A JOB TO DO. I HAD A PRICE TO PAY. MY LIFE HAD BEEN SALVAGED TO GIVE ME A CHANCE TO MAKE THINGS RIGHT, AND MY DEATH WAS GOING TO BE THE PAYMENT. I KNEW THE POWER OF DEATH, AND IT WAS ONLY WAY I COULD SEAL UP ORPHEUS AND THE SINISTERS FOREVER. I HAD TO BE OKAY WITH DEATH. MY RESOLVE STEADIED, EVEN AS MY HEART SQUEEZED TIGHTLY IN MY CHEST. I SUPPOSED IT HELPED, KNOWING I WAS NOT SUPPOSED TO BE ALIVE.

THE END

C. S. Johnson is the author of several young adult sci-fi and fantasy novels, including *The Starlight Chronicles* series, the *Once Upon a Princess* saga, and the *Divine Space Pirates* trilogy. With a gift for sarcasm and an apologetic heart, she currently lives in Atlanta with her family.

Please read on for a sample of *Beauty's Curse*, the first book in the Once Upon a Princes Sagas, a historical fantasy romance retelling of Sleeping Beauty, from C. S. Johnson.

Chapter 1 from

BEAUTY'S CURSE

PART I OF THE *ONCE UPON A PRINCESS* SAGA

✵   ✵   ✵   ✵

C. S. Johnson

1

She had never been one to waste her time; after all, she had so little of it left. But whether or not the weather cooperated with her was another matter entirely.

Rose looked up at the bleak sky, feeling the hood of her protective cloak sliding down from her face, exposing her nape at the end of her close-cropped hair. The wind tickled her skin, and rather than finding it charming and pleasant as she might have when she was younger, she found it taunting and terrifying.

Her gaze moved down from the crying skies to the sea, the rough and tumbling creature so keen on hogging every inch it could of the world's edge.

There was nothing to it, she decided. They would have to enter into the cavern during the rain. According to the map Ethan had found, the entrance to Titania's realm was not far down the cliff, and while it would be easier if the rain would stop and the tide would recede, Rose knew she could never count on life to make things easier for her if it could.

That was how Theo found her; looking down the edge of the cliffs, standing in the rain, and declaring all the world her enemy. No wonder she had insisted leaving the palace when she'd been thirteen, he thought. Even the grand palace would have demolished itself, had she been unable to fight her own way free of it. She was a warrior through and through.

Theo shook his head and pushed back the cover of his cloak. "I know that look," he muttered, coming up from behind her. "And the answer is no."

Rose would have normally grinned at the sight of her best friend following her out of the safety of the camp to talk. But ever since she and her group had finally found the location of the home of a powerful Fairy Queen, time seemed to crush into her a little bit more each day, pushing her into possible tomorrows long before her todays had finished.

She pursed her lips together. "Come on. I'm the princess, remember? I'm the one in command here, Theo."

He smiled at her. "You only pull rank when you know I'm right." Crossing his arms, he added, "It's only been two days, Rosary. We'll give it at least one more before we go barreling in."

He was not fooled by the calm look on her face; there would be a battle in getting her to agree.

He had known Rose–officially Princess Aurora Rosemarie Mohanagan of Rhone–for over ten years, ever since he arrived to work in the royal chapel, and he knew well her charms. It was impossible not to notice them, and knowing her well enough, it was impossible for him to fall for them–which, he knew, she both liked and hated on different occasions. Knowing her expressions just as well, Theo knew this time she hated it.

"Mary can protect us with a weather spell," she argued.

He had to admit, halfway begrudgingly, he admired her tenacity as she refused to back down. "Mary is still tired from our battle with the Eastern Warlords. We're all still tired, even you. The rest will be good for us. We have time enough for rest."

"No, I don't have time, Theo. My birthday is coming up." Frustration and fear crept into the pattern of her speech.

"And you can spare a day now, and we'll make up for it later."

"What if we don't?"

"You still have a whole year afterwards, Rosary." Patience melted away into concern at her words. He knew she was upset and afraid, and there was little he could do about it.

That was why he had come, though, wasn't it? The thought hit him with a disgruntled air. There were few reasons besides counsel and comfort that would cause one to bring a priest across continents and into battle. He was fortunate to have found a friend in the doomed princess of Rhone.

Theo watched as she started pacing, her knight's armor clanking quietly in tune with her stride. Time to reinforce the reason, he decided. "Sophia can't build much of a raft by the day's end. Why not send her to town with Virtue and some of the guards? She can surely go unnoticed here, even with your beast of a hawk, and she'll be able to see about a boat for tomorrow."

After a moment of silence, Rose smirked despite herself. "You and your logic," she muttered. She gave him a friendly punch on the shoulder. "Is there anything you don't use it for?"

"Some things," he replied, "that you know of well, and we share."

Rose felt a world pass between them inside his soft-spoken words, and found comfort in it. "Wanting revenge does tend to bind people together," Rose agreed, finally stopping in her tracks. She laid out her cloak and sat down on the ground. She pulled off her gloves, running her hands along the mossy ground. "Even people like you and me."

"You mean a princess and an orphan?"

She thought about it. "No, more than that," she said. "Not just that. More like someone cursed and someone raised by the church. But I guess that's wrong, too. You're not a priest. Not yet, anyway."

"All of mankind is cursed," Theo replied easily enough, sitting down next to her.

"I guess you sound like enough of one it's easy to forget," she teased back. She sighed. "It's not fair."

He looked over at her, and not for the first time, felt the pull of her presence. She was beautiful, even as she desperately tried to hide it. He didn't have the heart to tell her it was a waste of her time. With her chopped hair, the sunlight-kissed locks fluttered playfully, mysteriously; her eyes, as blue as the sky and unfathomable the sea, were framed by thick, sable lashes, and her lips, lips said to shame the reddest of roses, were as expressive and quirky as he knew her mind to be. Yes, he thought, life was not fair, even to the brightest among us.

Theo knew, having spent his adolescence in the palace, while Rose was angry at the curse placed on her at birth by the wicked fairy Magdalina, it was not the fear of a sleeping death that ailed her so much as the curse of relentless beauty. He smiled, recalling the day when an intended suitor, praising her with a song of her looks, had finally caused her perfected façade to fold.

Rose caught his smile. "What?" she snapped.

"I was thinking about the Prince of Crete," he said. "When he came, and you took his instrument—what was it? A mandolin or something?—and bashed him over the head with it, saying he should be ashamed he'd forgotten to mention how the pearly gates gleamed second only to your smile."

Rose laughed. "You remember his face? It was so red, I thought he was going to throw up."

"He looked like he'd just swallowed some pig slaw," Theo agreed. "But it was your mother's face which I still picture the best. She looked like she was going to murder you."

Rose giggled. "I guess that's one upside to Magdalina's curse. It's not like my mother's going to get away with murdering me. And neither will anyone else."

They fell back into an easy silence for a moment. Then Theo asked, "Is that why you like playing the mercenary knight?"

"It's not for just that reason," Rose assured him. She narrowed her gaze slyly in his direction. "You need the practice, remember?"

"Oh, I see now." Theo shook his head, trying to hide his grin. "Here I thought I was getting pretty good at being your squire."

"I told you months ago you were good enough to be a Rhonian knight," Rose reminded him. "Or did you just want to hear me say it again?"

"No, I wanted to hear you admit I'd beaten you in your battle testing." Theo smirked.

"Ha, it's always a riot with you. But anyway, Sophia's my official squire now."

"When she's not working on your armory."

"She likes doing that. And you know blacksmithing is very important to knights like us. She might as well practice and put it to use."

"She has been, and probably too much to really get in any knight training with the tournaments and the Eastern Warlord battles we've had recently."

"Which we might not have had to fight at all, if the Lead General hadn't been so demanding." Rose squeezed a handful of dirt and watched it slip through her fingers, a mixture of dust and mud. "The people in Greece are already taxed enough. He had some nerve demanding more. Even people like Ethan and Sophia's family deserve better."

Theo nodded. "And you work for it. One way or another."

"I like fighting, but I would rather see justice done, whether it's on the battlefield or in diplomacy," Rose said. "And if I get paid for it, all the better for us."

"I know. Since you feel you will never have it for yourself."

Rose shrugged. "I guess that's true. I mean, I know Magdalina wasn't invited to my party, but it's not exactly my fault for the war between the humans and the fairies, is it?"

Theo thought about the Magdust and the fairies who had died as the humans had captured and killed them and the retribution the humans faced. "No, it wasn't your fault."

"It wasn't fair of her to curse me."

"It wasn't fair of them to kill my family, either," Theo agreed.

"When I am Queen of Rhone, we'll find a way to deal with Magdalina and her magic," Rose vowed. "I just need to break the curse she placed on me first."

"Yes." A fierce protectiveness surged through him. How the world would change without Rose in it, he thought. How much his own world would change. Despite the fatigue of the journey, a renewed sense of determination wormed its way through Theo. He sighed.

"What's wrong?"

"Nothing, or maybe everything. I've decided you're right, so you win this time. We need to get down to Titania's terrarium and find a way to dispel the curse on you."

Rose allowed herself a rare moment of hesitation. She thought about how weary their battle finishing off the

Eastern Warlord had been, just a few days before, and how tired everyone in the party was, trying to get to the edge of the northern waters of the Aegean. She looked up at Theo, and saw the usual reserves of coolheaded strength, all wrapped up seamlessly in the sharpened angles of his face. He was her rock, the epitome of reason and faith mingled together. She knew he wouldn't have fought for the time off earlier if he hadn't thought it needed.

There was a warm glow that softened in his emerald eyes, as if he could read her thoughts. "It'll be fine, Rosary. There's not one of us that hasn't watched you shoulder someone else's pain these past four years, regardless of your curse or the amount of time you feel you have. And there's not one of us who wouldn't do the same for you, if you will let us."

She snorted and turned away, but his kind words struck her heart and brought a slim layer of grateful tears to her eyes.

"Let's go get Mary and see if Sophia can rig up a makeshift raft for us. If Ethan can get in on it, all the better. For all his map skills he seems to be more of an architect in the making." He stood up and reached down a hand for her.

Her palms felt smooth and strong in his own as he helped her to her feet, allowing Theo to feel the warmth of kinship.

"Okay. I thought I saw a fallen tree down there, by the edge of the forest. Sophia might be able to use that." Rose grinned. "You'll really let me win this time? Even against your better judgment? Despite your unconquerable logic?"

"There's a good reason you're 'Rosary' to me," Theo teased, chuckling a bit, yanking playfully at one of her sun-colored locks. "Go get everyone ready while I say my prayers."

Thank you for reading! Please leave a review for this book and check out www.csjohnson.me for other books and updates!